DOWN-ADOWN-DERRY

A Book of Fairy Poems by
WALTER DE LA MARE
with ❖ Illustrations ❖ by
DOROTHY P. LATHROP

DOWN-ADOWN-DERRY

A Book of Fairy Poems by
WALTER DE LA MARE
with ✠ Illustrations ✠ by
DOROTHY P. LATHROP

WILDSIDE PRESS

www.wildsidepress.com

CONTENTS

CONTENTS

FAIRIES

THE FAIRIES DANCING

I HEARD along the early hills,
  Ere yet the lark was risen up,
Ere yet the dawn with firelight fills
  The night-dew of the bramble-cup, —
I heard the fairies in a ring
  Sing as they tripped a lilting round
Soft as the moon on wavering wing.
  The starlight shook as if with sound,
As if with echoing, and the stars
  Prankt their bright eyes with trembling gleams
While red with war the gusty Mars
  Rained upon earth his ruddy beams.
He shone alone, low down the West,
  While I, behind a hawthorn-bush,
Watched on the fairies flaxen-tressed
  The fires of the morning flush.
Till, as a mist, their beauty died,
  Their singing shrill and fainter grew;
And daylight tremulous and wide
  Flooded the moorland through and through;
Till Urdon's copper weathercock
  Was reared in golden flame afar,
And dim from moonlit dreams awoke
  The towers and groves of Arroar.

3

DREAM-SONG

SUNLIGHT, moonlight,
Twilight, starlight —
Gloaming at the close of day,
And an owl calling,
Cool dews falling
In a wood of oak and may.

Lantern-light, taper-light,
Torchlight, no-light:
Darkness at the shut of day,
And lions roaring,
Their wrath pouring
In wild waste places far away.

Elf-light, bat-light,
Touchwood-light and toad-light,
And the sea a shimmering gloom of grey,
And a small face smiling
In a dream's beguiling
In a world of wonders far away.

4

A-TISHOO

"SNEEZE, Pretty, sneeze, Dainty,
  Else the Elves will have you sure,
Sneeze, Light-of-Seven-Bright-Candles,
  See they're tippeting at the door;
Their wee feet in measure falling,
All their little voices calling,
Calling, calling, calling, calling —
  Sneeze, or never come no more!"
        "A-tishoo!"

7

THE DOUBLE

I CURTSEYED to the dovecote.
   I curtseyed to the well.
I twirled me round and round about,
   The morning sweets to smell.
When out I came from spinning so,
   Lo, betwixt green and blue
Was the ghost of me — a Fairy Child —
   A-dancing — dancing, too.

Nought was of her wearing
   That is the earth's array.
Her thistledown feet beat airy fleet
   Yet set no blade astray.
The gossamer shining dews of June
   Showed grey against the green;
Yet never so much as a bird-claw print
   Of footfall to be seen.

Fading in the mounting sun
   That image soon did pine.
Fainter than moonlight thinned the locks
   That shone as clear as mine.
Vanished! Vanished! O, sad it is
   To spin and spin — in vain;
And never to see the ghost of me
   A-dancing there again.

THE UNFINISHED DREAM

RARE-SWEET the air in that unimagined country —
  My spirit had wandered far
From its weary body close-enwrapt in slumber
  Where its home and earth-friends are;

11

DOWN-ADOWN-DERRY

A milk-like air — and of light all abundance;
    And there a river clear
Painting the scene like a picture on its bosom,
    Green foliage drifting near.

No sign of life I saw, as I pressed onward,
    Fish, nor beast, nor bird,
Till I came to a hill clothed in flowers to its summit,
    Then shrill small voices I heard.

And I saw from concealment a company of elf-folk
    With faces strangely fair,
Talking their unearthly scattered talk together,
    A bind of green-grasses in their hair,

Marvellously gentle, feater far than children,
    In gesture, mien and speech,
Hastening onward in translucent shafts of sunshine,
    And gossiping each with each.

Straw-light their locks, on neck and shoulder falling,
    Faint of almond the silks they wore,
Spun not of worm, but as if inwoven of moonbeams
    And foam on rock-bound shore;

Like lank-legged grasshoppers in June-tide meadows,
    Amalillios of the day,
Hungrily gazed upon by me — a stranger,
    In unknown regions astray.

DOWN-ADOWN-DERRY

Yet, happy beyond words, I marked their sunlit faces,
    Stealing soft enchantment from their eyes,
Tears in my own confusing their small image,
    Harkening their bird-like cries.

They passed me, unseeing, a waft of flocking linnets;
    Sadly I fared on my way;
And came in my dream to a dreamlike habitation,
    Close-shut, festooned and grey.

Pausing, I gazed at the porch dust-still, vine-wreathèd,
    Worn the stone steps thereto,
Mute hung its bell, whence a stony head looked
        downward,
    Grey 'gainst the sky's pale-blue —

Strange to me: strange. . . .

DOWN-ADOWN-DERRY

THE HORN

HARK! is that a horn I hear,
   In cloudland winding sweet —
And bell-like clash of bridle-rein,
   And silver-shod light feet?

Is it the elfin laughter
   Of fairies riding faint and high,
Beneath the branches of the moon,
   Straying through the starry sky?

Is it in the globèd dew
   Such sweet melodies may fall?
Wood and valley — all are still,
   Hushed the shepherd's call.

14

THE THREE BEGGARS

'TWAS autumn daybreak gold and wild,
  While past St. Ann's grey tower they shuffled,
Three beggars spied a fairy-child
  In crimson mantle muffled.

17

DOWN-ADOWN-DERRY

The daybreak lighted up her face
   All pink, and sharp, and emerald-eyed;
She looked on them a little space,
   And shrill as hautboy cried: —

"O three tall footsore men of rags
   Which walking this gold morn I see,
What will ye give me from your bags
   For fairy kisses three?"

The first, that was a reddish man,
   Out of his bundle takes a crust:
"La, by the tombstones of St. Ann,
   There's fee, if fee ye must!"

The second, that was a chestnut man,
   Out of his bundle draws a bone:
"Lo, by the belfry of St. Ann,
   And all my breakfast gone!"

The third, that was a yellow man,
   Out of his bundle picks a groat,
"La, by the Angel of St. Ann,
   And I must go without."

That changeling, lean and icy-lipped,
   Touched crust, and bone, and groat, and lo!
Beneath her finger taper-tipped
   The magic all ran through.

18

DOWN-ADOWN-DERRY

Instead of crust a peacock pie,
 Instead of bone sweet venison,
Instead of groat a white lily
 With seven blooms thereon.

And each fair cup was deep with wine:
 Such was the changeling's charity,
The sweet feast was enough for nine,
 But not too much for three.

O toothsome meat in jelly froze!
 O tender haunch of elfin stag!
O rich the odour that arose!
 O plump with scraps each bag!

There, in the daybreak gold and wild,
 Each merry-hearted beggar man
Drank deep unto the fairy child,
 And blessed the good St. Ann.

THE STRANGER

In the nook of a wood where a pool freshed with dew
Glassed, daybreak till evening, blue sky glimpsing through
Then a star; or a slip of May-moon silver-white,
Thridding softly aloof the quiet of night,
    Was a thicket of flowers.

Willow herb, mint, pale speedwell and rattle
Water hemlock and sundew — to the wind's tittle-tattle
They nodded, dreamed, swayed in jocund delight,
In beauty and sweetness arrayed, still and bright.
By turn scampered rabbit; trotted fox; bee and bird
Paused droning, sang shrill, and the fair water stirred.
Plashed green frog, or some brisk little flickering fish —
Gudgeon, stickleback, minnow—set the ripples a-swish.

A lone pool, a pool grass-fringed, crystal-clear:
Deep, placid, and cool in the sweet of the year;
Edge-parched when the sun to the Dog Days drew near;
And with winter's bleak rime hard as glass, robed in snow,
The whole wild-wood sleeping, and nothing a-blow
But the wind from the North — bringing snow.

That is all. Save that one long, sweet, June night-tide
    straying,
The harsh hemlock's pale umbelliferous bloom
Tenting nook, dense with fragrance and secret with gloom,
In a beaming of moon-colored light faintly raying,
On buds orbed with dew phosphorescently playing,
Came a Stranger — still-footed, feat-fingered, clear face
Unhumanly lovely: . . . and supped in that place.

THE RUIN

WHEN the last colours of the day
Have from their burning ebbed away,
About that ruin, cold and lone,
The cricket shrills from stone to stone;
And scattering o'er its darkened green,
Bands of the fairies may be seen,
Chattering like grasshoppers, their feet
Dancing a thistledown dance round it:
While the great gold of the mild moon
Tinges their tiny acorn shoon.

23

THE FAIRY IN WINTER

THERE was a Fairy — flake of winter —
Who, when the snow came, whispering, Silence,
Sister crystal to crystal sighing,
Making of meadow argent palace,
   Night a star-sown solitude,
Cried 'neath her frozen eaves, "I burn here!"

Wings diaphanous, beating bee-like,
Wand within fingers, locks enspangled,
Icicle foot, lip sharp as scarlet,
She lifted her eyes in her pitch-black hollow —
Green as stalks of weeds in water —
Breathed: stirred.

Rilled from her heart the ichor, coursing,
Flamed and awoke her slumbering magic.
Softlier than moth's her pinions trembled;
Out into blackness, light-like, she flittered,
Leaving her hollow cold, forsaken.

In air, o'er crystal, rang twangling night-wind.
Bare, rimed pine-woods murmured lament.

24

SLEEPYHEAD

As I lay awake in the white moonlight
I heard a faint singing in the wood,
　　"Out of bed,
　　Sleepyhead,
　　Put your white foot, now;

DOWN-ADOWN-DERRY

Here are we
Beneath the tree
Singing round the root now."

I looked out of window, in the white moonlight,
The leaves were like snow in the wood —
"Come away,
Child, and play
Light with the gnomies;
In a mound,
Green and round,
That's where their home is.

"Honey sweet,
Curds to eat,
Cream and frumenty,
Shells and beads,
Poppy seeds,
You shall have plenty."

But, as soon as I stooped in the dim moonlight
To put on my stocking and my shoe,
The sweet shrill singing echoed faintly away,
And the grey of the morning peeped through,
And instead of the gnomies there came a red robin
To sing of the buttercups and dew.

SAM'S THREE WISHES; or LIFE'S LITTLE WHIRLIGIG

"I'M thinking and thinking," said old Sam Shore,
"'Twere somebody *knocking* I heard at the door."

From the clock popped the cuckoo and cuckooed out
    eight,
As there in his chair he wondering sate . . .

29

DOWN-ADOWN-DERRY

"There's no one I knows on would come so late,
A-clicking the latch of an empty house
With nobbut inside 'un but me and a mouse. . . .
Maybe a-waking in sleep I be,
And 'twere out of a dream came that tapping to
    me."
At length he cautiously rose, and went,
And with thumb upon latch awhile listening bent,
Then slowly drew open the door.   And behold!
There stood a Fairy! — all green and gold,
Mantled up warm against dark and cold,
And smiling up into his candle shine,
Lips like wax, and cheeks like wine,
As saucy and winsome a thing to see
As are linden buds on a linden tree.

Stock-still in the doorway stood simple Sam,
A-ducking his head, with "Good-e'en to 'ee, Ma'am."

Dame Fairy she nods, and cries clear and sweet,
"'Tis a *very* good-e'en, sir, when such folks meet.
I know thee, Sam, though thou wist not of me,
And I'm come in late gloaming to speak with thee;
Though my eyes do dazzle at glint of your rush,
All under this pretty green fuchsia bush."

Sam ducked once more, smiling simple and slow.
Like the warbling of birds her words did flow,
And she laughed, very merry, to see how true
Shone the old man's kindness his courtesy through.

And she nodded her head, and the stars on high
Sparkled down on her smallness from out of the sky.

"A friend is a friend, Sam, and wonderful pleasant,
And I'm come for old sake's sake to bring thee a present.
Three wishes, three wishes are thine, Sam Shore,
Just three wishes — and wish no more,
All for because, ruby-ripe to see,
The pixy-pears burn in yon hawthorn tree,
And your old milch cow, wheresoever she goes
Never crops over the fairy-knowes.
Ay, Sam, thou art old and thy house is lone,
But there's Potencies round thee, and here is one!"

Poor Sam, he stared: and the star o'erhead
A shimmering light on the elm-tops shed.
Like rilling of water her voice rang sweet,
And the night-wind sighed at the sound of it.
He frowned — glanced back at the empty grate,
And shook very slowly his grey old pate:
"Three wishes, my dear! Why, I scarcely knows
Which be my crany and which my toes!
But I thank 'ee, Ma'am, kindly, and this I'd say,
That the night of your passing is Michaelmas Day;
And if it were company come on a sudden,
Why, I'd ax for a fat goose to fry in the oven!"

And lo, and forsooth! as the words he was uttering,
A rich puff of air set his candle a-guttering,

31

And there rose in the kitchen a sizzling and sputtering,
With a crackling of sparks and of flames a great
    fluttering,
And — of which here could not be two opinions —
A smoking-hot savour of sage and onions.
Beam, wall and flagstones the kitchen was lit,
Every dark corner and cranny of it
With the blaze from the hearthstone.   Copper and brass
Winked back the winking of platter and glass.
And a wonderful squeaking of mice went up
At the smell of a Michaelmas supper to sup —
Unctuous odours that wreathed and swirled
Where'er frisked a whisker or mouse-tail twirled,
While out of the chimney up into the night
That ne'er-to-be-snuffed-too-much smoke took flight.
"That's one," says the Fairy, finger on thumb,
"So now, Mister Sam, there's but two to come!"
She leaned her head sidelong; she lifted her chin,
With a twinkling of eye from the radiance within.
Poor Sam stood astounded; he says, says he,
"I *wish* my old Mother was back with me,
For if there was one thing she couldn't refuse
'Twas a sweet thick slice from the breast of a goose."
But his cheek grew stiff and his eyes stared bright,
For there, on her stick, pushing out of the night,
Tap-tapping along, herself and no other,
Came who but the shape of his dear old Mother!
Straight into the kitchen she hastened and went,
Her breath coming quick as if all but spent.

"Why, Sam," says she, "the bird be turning,
For my nose tells I that the skin's a-burning!"
And down at the oven the ghost of her sat
And basted the goose with the boiling fat.

"Oho," cries the Fairy, sweet and small,
"Another wish gone will leave nothing at all."
And Sam sighs, "Bless 'ee, Ma'am, keep the other,
There's nowt that I want now I have my Mother."
But the Fairy laughs softly, and says, says she,
"There's one wish left, Sam, I promised 'ee three.
Hasten your wits, the hour creeps on,
There's calling afield and I'm soon to be gone.
Soon as haps midnight the cocks will crow
And me to the gathering and feasting must go."

Sam gazed at his Mother —withered and wan,
The rose in her cheek, her bright hair, gone,
And her poor old back bent double with years —
And he scarce could speak for the salt, salt tears.
"Well, well," he says, "I'm unspeakable glad:
But — it bain't quite the same as when I was a lad.
There's joy and there's joy, Ma'am, but to tell 'ee
    the truth
There's none can compare with the joy of one's youth.
And if it was possible, how could I choose
But be back in boy's breeches to eat the goose;
And all the old things — and my Mother the most,
To shine again real as my own gatepost.
What wouldn't I give, too, to see again wag

DOWN-ADOWN-DERRY

The dumpity tail of my old dog, Shag!
Your kindness, Ma'am, but all wishing was vain
Unless us can both be young again."
A shrill, faint laughter from nowhere came . . .
Empty the dark in the candle-flame. . . .

And there stood our Sam, about four foot high,
Snub nose, shock hair, and round blue eye.
Breeches and braces and coat of him too,
Shirt on his back, and each clodhopping shoe
Had shrunk to a nicety — button and hem
To fit the small Sammie tucked up into them.

There was his Mother, too; smooth, dear cheek,
Lips as smooth as a blackbird's beak,
Pretty arched eyebrows, the daintiest nose —
While the smoke of the baking deliciously rose.

"Come, Sammie," she cries, "your old Mammikin's
      joy,
Climb up on your stool, supper's ready, my boy.
Bring in the candle, and shut out the night;
There's goose, baked taties and cabbage to bite.
Why, bless the wee lamb, he's all shiver and shake,
And you'd think from the look of him scarcely awake!
If 'ee glour wi' those eyes, Sam, so dark and round,
The elves will away with 'ee, I'll be bound!"
So Sam and his Mother by wishes three
Were made just as happy as happy can be.
And there — with a bumpity tail to wag —

DOWN-ADOWN-DERRY

Sat laughing, with tongue out, their old dog, Shag.
To clatter of patter, bones, giblets and juice,
Between them they ate up the whole of the goose.

But time is a river for ever in flow,
The weeks went by as the weeks must go.
Soon fifty-two to a year did grow.
The long years passed, one after another,
Making older and older our Sam and his Mother;
And, alas and alack, with nine of them gone,
Poor Shag lay asleep again under a stone.
And a sorrowful dread would sometimes creep
Into Sam's dreams, as he lay asleep,
That his Mother was lost, and away he'd fare,
Calling her, calling her, everywhere,
In dark, in rain, by roads unknown,
Under echoing hills, and alone, alone.
What bliss in the morning to wake and se
The sun shining green in the linden tree,
And out of that dream's dark shadowiness
To slip in on his Mother and give her a kiss,
And go whistling off in the dew to hear
The thrushes all mocking him, sweet and clear.

Still, moon after moon from heaven above
Shone on Mother and son, and made light of love.
Her roses faded, her pretty brown hair
Had sorrowful grey in it everywhere.
And at last she died, and was laid to rest,

35

DOWN-A DOWN-DERRY

Her tired hands crossed on her shrunken breast.
And Sam, now lonely, lived on and on
Till most of his workaday life seemed gone.

Yet spring came again with its green and blue,
And presently summer's wild roses too,
Pinks, Sweet William, and sops-in-wine,
Blackberry, lavender, eglantine.
And when these had blossomed and gone their way,
'Twas apples, and daisies and Michaelmas Day —
Yes, spider-webs, dew, and haws in the may,
And seraphs singing in Michaelmas Day.

Sam worked all morning and *couldn't* get rest
For a kind of a feeling of grief in his breast.
And yet, not grief, but something more
Like the thought that what happens has happened
    before.
He fed the chickens, he fed the sow,
On a three-legged stool sate down to the cow,
With a pail 'twixt his legs in the green in the meadow,
Under the elm trees' lengthening shadow;
And woke at last with a smile and a sigh
To find he had milked his poor Jingo dry.

As dusk set in, even the birds did seem
To be calling and calling from out of a dream.
He chopped up kindling, shut up his shed,
In a bucket of well-water soused his head ·

DOWN-ADOWN-DERRY

To freshen his eyes up a little and make
The drowsy old wits of him wider awake.
As neat as a womanless creature is able
He swept up his hearthstone and laid the table.
And then o'er his platter and mug, if you please,
Sate gloomily gooming at loaf and cheese —
Gooming and gooming as if the mere sight
Of his victuals could satisfy appetite!
And the longer and longer he looked at them
The slimmer slimmed upward his candle flame,
Blue in the air. And when squeaked a mouse
'Twas loud as a trump in the hush of the house.
Then, sudden, a soft little wind puffed by,
'Twixt the thick-thatched roof and the star-sown sky;
And died. And then
That deep, dead, wonderful silence again.

Then — soft as a rattle a-counting her seeds
In the midst of a tangle of withered-up weeds —
Came a faint, faint knocking, a rustle like silk,
And a breath at the keyhole as soft as milk —
Still as the flit of a moth. And then . . .
That infinitesimal knocking again.

Sam lifted his chin from his fists. He listened.
His wandering eyes in the candle glistened.
Then slowly, slowly, rolled round by degrees —
And there sat a mouse on the top of his cheese.
He stared at this Midget, and it at him,

37

DOWN–A DOWN–DERRY

Over the edge of his mug's round rim,
And — as if it were Christian — he says, "Did 'ee hear
A faint little tap-tap-tap-tapping, my dear?
You was at supper and me in a maze
'Tis dark for a caller in these lone days,
There's nowt in the larder.   We're both of us old.
And all of my loved ones sleep under the mould,
And yet — and yet — as I've told 'ee before . . ."

But if Sam's story you'd read to the end,
Turn back to page 1, and press onward, dear friend;
Yes, if you would stave the last note of this song,
Turn back to page primus, and warble along!
For all sober records of life (come to write 'em),
Are bound to continue — well — ad infinitum!

PEAK AND PUKE

FROM his cradle in the glamourie
They have stolen my wee brother,
Roused a changeling in his swaddlings
For to fret mine own poor mother.
Pules it in the candle light
Wi' a cheek so lean and white,
Chinkling up its eyne so wee,
Wailing shrill at her an' me.

39

DOWN-ADOWN-DERRY

It we'll neither rock nor tend
Till the Silent Silent send,
Lapping in their waesome arms
Him they stole with spells and charms,
Till they take this changeling creature
Back to its own fairy nature —
Cry! Cry! as long as may be,
Ye shall ne'er be woman's baby!

THE CHANGELING

"AHOY, and ahoy!"
　'Twixt mocking and merry —
"Ahoy and ahoy, there,
　Young man of the ferry!"
She stood on the steps
　In the watery gloom —
That Changeling — "Ahoy, there!"
　She called him to come.
He came on the green wave,
　He came on the grey,
Where stooped that sweet lady
　That still summer's day.
He fell in a dream
　Of her beautiful face,
As she sat on the thwart
　And smiled in her place.
No echo his oar woke,
　Float silent did they,
Past low-grazing cattle
　In the sweet of the hay.
And still in a dream
　At her beauty sat he,
Drifting stern foremost
　Down — down to the sea.

41

DOWN – A DOWN – DERRY

Come you, then: call,
　When the twilight apace
Brings shadow to brood
　On the loveliest face;
You shall hear o'er the water
　Ring faint in the grey —
"Ahoy, and ahoy, there!"
　And tremble away;
"Ahoy, and ahoy! . . ."
　And tremble away.

LOB LIE BY THE FIRE

HE squats by the fire
  On his three-legged stool,
When all in the house
  With slumber are full.

45

DOWN-ADOWN-DERRY

And he warms his great hands,
  Hanging loose from each knee.
And he whistles as soft
  As the night wind at sea.

For his work now is done;
  All the water is sweet;
He has turned each brown loaf,
  And breathed magic on it.

The milk in the pan,
  And the bacon on beam
He has "spelled" with his thumb,
  And bewitched has the dream.

Not a mouse, not a moth,
  Not a spider but sat,
And quaked as it wondered
  What next he'd be at.

But his heart, O, his heart —
  It belies his great nose;
And at gleam of his eye
  Not a soul would suppose

He had stooped with great thumbs,
  And big thatched head,
To tuck his small mistress
  More snugly in bed.

46

DOWN-A DOWN-DERRY

Who would think, now, a throat
  So lank and so thin
Might make birds seem to warble
  In the dream she is in!

Now hunched by the fire,
  While the embers burn low,
He nods until daybreak,
  And at daybreak he'll go.

Soon the first cock will 'light
  From his perch and point high
His beak at the Ploughboy
  Grown pale in the sky;

And crow will he shrill;
  Then, meek as a mouse,
Lob will rouse up and shuffle
  Straight out of the house.

His supper for breakfast;
  For wages his work;
And to warm his great hands
  Just an hour in the mirk.

BLUEBELLS

WHERE the bluebells and the wind are,
  Fairies in a ring I spied,
And I heard a little linnet
  Singing near beside.

Where the primrose and the dew are —
  Soon were sped the fairies all:
Only now the green turf freshens,
  And the linnets call.

THE HONEY ROBBERS

THERE were two Fairies, Gimmul and Mel,
Loved Earth Man's honey passing well;
Oft at the hives of his tame bees
They would their sugary thirst appease.
When even began to darken to night,
They would hie along in the fading light,
With elf-locked hair and scarlet lips,

51

DOWN-ADOWN-DERRY

And small stone knives to slit the skeps,
So softly not a bee inside
Should hear the woven straw divide.
And then with sly and greedy thumbs
Would rifle the sweet honeycombs.
And drowsily drone to drone would say,
"A cold, cold wind blows in this way";
And the great Queen would turn her head
From face to face, astonishèd,
And, though her maids with comb and brush
Would comb and soothe and whisper, "Hush!"
About the hive would shrilly go
A keening — keening, to and fro;
At which those robbers 'neath the trees
Would taunt and mock the honey-bees,
And through their sticky teeth would buzz
Just as an angry hornet does.
And when this Gimmul and this Mel
Had munched and sucked and swilled their fill,
Or ever Man's first cock could crow
Back to their Faërie Mounds they'd go.
Edging across the twilight air,
Thieves of a guise remotely fair.

BERRIES

THERE was an old woman
    Went blackberry picking
Along the hedges
    From Weep to Wicking.
Half a pottle —
    No more she had got,
When out steps a Fairy
    From her green grot;
And says, "Well, Jill,
    Would 'ee pick 'ee mo?"
And Jill, she curtseys,
    And looks just so.
"Be off," says the Fairy,
    "As quick as you can,
Over the meadows
    To the little green lane,
That dips to the hayfields
    Of Farmer Grimes:
I've berried those hedges
    A score of times;
Bushel on bushel
    I'll promise 'ee, Jill,
This side of supper
    If 'ee pick with a will."

55

DOWN-ADOWN-DERRY

She glints very bright,
  And speaks her fair;
Then lo, and behold!
  She has faded in air.

Be sure old Goodie
  She trots betimes
Over the meadows
  To Farmer Grimes.
And never was queen
  With jewellry rich
As those same hedges
  From twig to ditch;
Like Dutchmen's coffers,
  Fruit, thorn, and flower —
They shone like William
  And Mary's bower.
And be sure Old Goodie
  Went back to Weep,
So tired with her basket
  She scarce could creep.
When she comes in the dusk
  To her cottage door,
There's Towser wagging
  As never before,
To see his Missus
  So glad to be
Come from her fruit-picking
  Back to he.

DOWN-ADOWN-DERRY

As soon as next morning
  Dawn was grey,
The pot on the hob
  Was simmering away;
And all in a stew
  And a hugger-mugger
Towser and Jill
  A-boiling of sugar,
And the dark clear fruit
  That from Faërie came,
For syrup and jelly
  And blackberry jam.

Twelve jolly gallipots
  Jill put by;
And one little teeny one,
  One inch high;
And that she's hidden
  A good thumb deep,
Half way over
  From Wicking to Weep.

DOWN-ADOWN-DERRY

HAPPY, HAPPY IT IS TO BE

"HAPPY, happy it is to be
Where the greenwood hangs o'er the dark blue sea;
To roam in the moonbeams clear and still
And dance with the elves
Over dale and hill;
To taste their cups, and with them roam
The field for dewdrops and honeycomb.
Climb then, and come, as quick as you can,
And dwell with the fairies, Elizabeth Ann!

"Never, never, comes tear or sorrow,
In the mansions old where the fairies dwell;
But only the harping of their sweet harp-strings,
And the lonesome stroke of a distant bell,
Where upon hills of thyme and heather,
The shepherd sits with his wandering sheep;
And the curlew wails, and the skylark hovers
Over the sand where the conies creep;
Climb then, and come, as quick as you can,
And dwell with the fairies, Elizabeth Ann!"

58

DOWN-ADOWN-DERRY

THE MIDDEN'S SONG

"BUBBLE, Bubble,
   Swim to see
Oh, how beautiful
   I be.

"Fishes, Fishes,
   Finned and fine,
What's your gold
   Compared with mine?

"Why, then, has
   Wise Tishnar made
One so lovely,
   Yet so sad?

"Lone am I,
   And can but make
A little song,
   For singing's sake."

Reprinted by permission from *The Three Mulla-Mulgars*, Alfred A. Knopf, New York, 1919.

ALL BUT BLIND

ALL but blind
  In his chambered hole
Gropes for worms
  The four-clawed Mole.

All but blind
  In the evening sky
The hooded Bat
  Twirls softly by.

All but blind
  In the burning day
The Barn-Owl blunders
  On her way.

And blind as are
  These three to me,
So, blind to Some-one
  I must be.

THE MOCKING FAIRY

"WON'T you look out of your window, Mrs. Gill?"
 Quoth the Fairy, nidding, nodding in the garden;
"*Can't* you look out of your window, Mrs. Gill?"
 Quoth the Fairy, laughing softly in the garden;
But the air was still, the cherry boughs were still,
And the ivy-tod 'neath the empty sill,
And never from her window looked out Mrs. Gill
 On the Fairy shrilly mocking in the garden.

"What have they done with you, you poor Mrs. Gill?"
 Quoth the Fairy, brightly glancing in the garden;
"Where have they hidden you, you poor old Mrs. Gill?"
 Quoth the Fairy dancing lightly in the garden;
But night's faint veil now wrapped the hill,
Stark 'neath the stars stood the dead-still Mill,
And out of her cold cottage never answered Mrs. Gill
 The Fairy mimbling mambling in the garden.

69

DOWN-ADOWN-DERRY

Down-adown-derry,
  Sweet Annie Maroon,
Gathering daisies
  In the meadows of Doone,
Hears a shrill piping,
  Elflike and free,
Where the waters go brawling
  In rills to the sea;
    Singing down-adown-derry.

Down-adown-derry,
  Sweet Annie Maroon,
Through the green grasses
  Peeps softly; and soon
Spies under green willows
  A fairy whose song
Like the smallest of bubbles
  Floats bobbing along;
    Singing down-adown-derry.

DOWN-ADOWN-DERRY

Down-adown-derry,
  Her cheeks were like wine,
Her eyes in her wee face
  Like water-sparks shine,
Her niminy fingers
  Her sleek tresses preen,
The which in the combing
  She peeps out between;
    Singing down-adown-derry.

Down-adown-derry,
  Shrill, shrill was her tune: —
"Come to my water-house,
  Annie Maroon:
Come in your dimity,
  Ribbon on head,
To wear siller seaweed
  And coral instead";
    Singing down-adown-derry.

"Down-adown-derry,
  Lean fish of the sea,
Bring lanthorns for feasting
  The gay Faërie;
'Tis sand for the dancing,
  A music all sweet
In the water-green gloaming
  For thistledown feet";
    Singing down-adown-derry.

71

DOWN-ADOWN-DERRY

Down-adown-derry,
    Sweet Annie Maroon
Looked large on the fairy
    Curled wan as the moon
And all the grey ripples
    To the Mill racing by,
With harps and with timbrels
    Did ringing reply;
        Singing down-adown-derry.

"Down-adown-derry,"
    Sang the Fairy of Doone,
Piercing the heart
    Of Sweet Annie Maroon;
And lo! when like roses
    The clouds of the sun
Faded at dusk, gone
    Was Annie Maroon;
        Singing down-adown-derry.

Down-adown-derry,
    The daisies are few;
Frost twinkles powdery
    In haunts of the dew;
And only the robin
    Perched on a thorn,
Can comfort the heart
    Of a father forlorn;
        Singing down-adown-derry.

72

DOWN-ADOWN-DERRY

Down-adown-derry,
    There's snow in the air;
Ice where the lily
    Bloomed waxen and fair;
He may call o'er the water,
    Cry — cry through the Mill,
But Annie Maroon, alas!
    Answer ne'er will;
        Singing down-adown-derry.

WITCHES AND WITCHCRAFT

THE HARE

In the black furrow of a field
  I saw an old witch-hare this night;
And she cocked a lissome ear,
  And she eyed the moon so bright,
And she nibbled of the green;
  And I whispered "Wh-s-st! witch-hare,"
Away like a ghostie o'er the field
  She fled, and left the moonlight there.

I SAW THREE WITCHES

I SAW three witches
That bowed down like barley,

DOWN-ADOWN-DERRY

And straddled their brooms 'neath a louring sky,
And, mounting a storm-cloud,
Aloft on its margin,
Stood black in the silver as up they did fly.

I saw three witches
That mocked the poor sparrows
They carried in cages of wicker along,
Till a hawk from his eyrie
Swooped down like an arrow,
Smote on the cages, and ended their song.

I saw three witches
That sailed in a shallop,
All turning their heads with a snickering smile,
Till a bank of green osiers
Concealed their grim faces,
Though I heard them lamenting for many a mile.

I saw three witches
Asleep in a valley,
Their heads in a row, like stones in a flood,
Till the moon, creeping upward,
Looked white through the valley,
And turned them to bushes in bright scarlet bud.

THE ISLE OF LONE

THREE dwarfs there were which lived in an isle,
  And the name of that Isle was Lone,
And the names of the dwarfs were Alliolyle,
  Lallerie, Muziomone.

Alliolyle was green of een,
  Lallerie light of locks,
Muziomone was mild of mien,
  As ewes in April flocks.

81

DOWN-A DOWN-DERRY

Their house was small and sweet of the sea,
    And pale as the Malmsey wine;
Their bowls were three, and their beds were three,
    And their nightcaps white were nine.

Their beds they were made of the holly-wood,
    Their combs of the tortoise's shell,
Three basins of silver in corners there stood,
    And three little ewers as well.

Green rushes, green rushes lay thick on the floor,
    For light beamed a gobbet of wax;
There were three wooden stools for whatever they wore
    On their humpity-dumpity backs.

So each would lie on a drowsy pillow
    And watch the moon in the sky —
And hear the parrot scream to the billow,
    The billow roar reply:

Parrots of sapphire and sulphur and amber,
    Scarlet, and flame, and green,
While five-foot apes did scramble and clamber,
    In the feathery-tufted treen.

All night long with bubbles a-glisten
    The ocean cried under the moon,
Till ape and parrot, too sleepy to listen,
    To sleep and slumber were gone.

DOWN-ADOWN-DERRY

Then from three small beds the dark hours' while
   In a house in the Island of Lone
Rose the snoring of Lallerie, Alliolyle,
   The snoring of Muziomone.

But soon as ever came peep of sun
   On coral and feathery tree,
Three nightcapped dwarfs to the surf would run
   And soon were a-bob in the sea.

At six they went fishing, at nine they snared
   Young foxes in the dells,
At noon on sweet berries and honey they fared,
   And blew in their twisted shells.

Dark was the sea they gambolled in,
   And thick with silver fish,
Dark as green glass blown clear and thin
   To be a monarch's dish.

They sate to sup in a jasmine bower,
   Lit pale with flies of fire,
Their bowls the hue of the iris-flower,
   And lemon their attire.

Sweet wine in little cups they sipped,
   And golden honeycomb
Into their bowls of cream they dipped,
   Whipt light and white as foam.

83

DOWN–ADOWN–DERRY

Now Alliolyle, where the sand-flower blows,
   Taught three old apes to sing —
Taught three old apes to dance on their toes
   And caper around in a ring.

They yelled them hoarse and they croaked them sweet,
   They twirled them about and around,
To the noise of their voices they danced with their feet,
   They stamped with their feet on the ground.

But down to the shore skipped Lallerie,
   His parrot on his thumb,
And the twain they scritched in mockery,
   While the dancers go and come.

And, alas! in the evening, rosy and still,
   Light-haired Lallerie
Bitterly quarrelled with Alliolyle
   By the yellow-sanded sea.

The rising moon swam sweet and large
   Before their furious eyes,
And they rolled and rolled to the coral marge
   Where the surf for ever cries.

Too late, too late, comes Muziomone:
   Clear in the clear green sea
Alliolyle lies not alone,
   But clasped with Lallerie.

DOWN-ADOWN-DERRY

He blows on his shell plaintive notes;
  Ape, parraquito, bee
Flock where a shoe on the salt wave floats, —
  The shoe of Lallerie.

He fetches nightcaps, one and nine,
  Grey apes he dowers three,
His house as fair as the Malmsey wine
  Seems sad as cypress-tree.

Three bowls he brims with sweet honeycomb
  To feast the bumble bees,
Saying, "O bees, be this your home,
  For grief is on the seas!"

He sate him lone in a coral grot,
  At the flowing in of the tide;
When ebbed the billow, there was not,
  Save coral, aught beside.

So hairy apes in three white beds,
  And nightcaps, one and nine,
On moonlit pillows lay three heads
  Bemused with dwarfish wine.

A tomb of coral, the dirge of bee,
  The grey apes' guttural groan
For Alliolyle, for Lallerie,
  For thee, O Muziomone!

SUNK LYONESSE

IN sea-cold Lyonesse,
  When the Sabbath eve shafts down
On the roofs, walls, belfries
  Of the foundered town,
The Nereids pluck their lyres
  Where the green translucency beats,
And with motionless eyes at gaze
  Make minstrelsy in the streets.

The ocean water stirs
  In salt-worn casemate and porch
Plies the blunt-snouted fish
  With fire in his skull for torch.
And the ringing wires resound;
  And the unearthly lovely weep,
In lament of the music they make
  In the sullen courts of sleep.

Whose marble flowers bloom for aye,
  And — lapped by the moon-guiled tide —
Mock their carver with heart of stone,
  Caged in his stone-ribbed side.

86

SLEEPING BEAUTY

THE scent of bramble fills the air,
　Amid her folded sheets she lies,
The gold of evening in her hair,
　The blue of morn shut in her eyes.

89

DOWN-ADOWN-DERRY

How many a changing moon hath lit
   The unchanging roses of her face!
Her mirror ever broods on it
   In silver stillness of the days.

Oft flits the moth on filmy wings
   Into his solitary lair;
Shrill evensong the cricket sings
   From some still shadow in her hair.

In heat, in snow, in wind, in flood,
   She sleeps in lovely loneliness,
Half-folded like an April bud
   On winter-haunted trees.

BEWITCHED

I HAVE heard a lady this night,
  Lissom and jimp and slim,
Calling me — calling me over the heather,
  .'Neath the beech boughs dusk and dim.

DOWN-ADOWN-DERRY

I have followed a lady this night,
    Followed her far and lone,
Fox and adder and weasel know
    The ways that we have gone.

I sit at my supper 'mid honest faces,
    And crumble my crust and say
Nought in the long-drawn drawl of the voices
    Talking the hours away.

I'll go to my chamber under the gable,
    And the moon will lift her light
In at my lattice from over the moorland
    Hollow and still and bright.

And I know she will shine on a lady of witchcraft,
    Gladness and grief to see,
Who has taken my heart with her nimble fingers,
    Calls in my dreams to me:

Who has led me a dance by dell and dingle
    My human soul to win,
Made me a changeling to my own, own mother,
    A stranger to my kin.

THE ENCHANTED HILL

FROM height of noon, remote and still,
The sun shines on the empty hill.
No mist, no wind, above, below;
No living thing strays to and fro.
No bird replies to bird on high,
Cleaving the skies with echoing cry.
Like dreaming water, green and wan,
Glassing the snow of mantling swan,
Like a clear jewel encharactered
With secret symbol of line and word,
Asheen, unruffled, slumbrous, still,
The sunlight streams on the empty hill.

But soon as Night's dark shadows ride
Across its shrouded Eastern side,
When at her kindling, clear and full,
Star beyond star stands visible;
Then course pale phantoms, fleet-foot deer
Lap of its waters icy-clear;
Mounts the large moon, and pours her beams
On bright-fish-flashing, singing streams;
Voices re-echo; coursing by,
Horsemen, like clouds, wheel silently.

93

DOWN-ADOWN-DERRY

Glide then from out their pitch-black lair
Beneath the dark's ensilvered arch,
Witches becowled into the air;
And iron pine and emerald larch,
Tents of delight for ravished bird,
Are by loud music thrilled and stirred.
Winging the light, with silver feet,
Beneath their bowers of fragrance met,
In dells of rose and meadowsweet,
In mazed dance the fairies flit;
While drives his share the Ploughman high
Athwart the daisy-powdered sky:
Till far away, in thickening dew,
Piercing the Eastern shadows through
Rilling in crystal clear and still,
Light 'gins to tremble on the hill.
And like a mist on faint winds borne,
Silent, forlorn, wells up the morn.
Then the broad sun with burning beams
Steeps slope and peak and gilded streams.
Then no foot stirs; the brake shakes not;
Soundless and wet in its green grot
As if asleep, the leaf hangs limp;
The white dews drip untrembling down,
From bough to bough, orblike, unblown;
And in strange quiet, shimmering and still,
Morning enshrines the empty hill.

THE RIDE-BY-NIGHTS

Up on their brooms the Witches stream,
Crooked and black in the crescent's gleam;

97

DOWN-ADOWN-DERRY

One foot high, and one foot low,
Bearded, cloaked, and cowled, they go.
'Neath Charlie's Wane they twitter and tweet,
And away they swarm 'neath the Dragon's feet.
With a whoop and a flutter they swing and sway,
And surge pell-mell down the Milky Way.
Betwixt the legs of the glittering Chair
They hover and squeak in the empty air.
Then round they swoop past the glimmering Lion
To where Sirius barks behind huge Orion;
Up, then, and over to wheel amain,
Under the silver, and home again.

OFF THE GROUND

THREE jolly Farmers
  Once bet a pound
Each dance the others would
  Off the ground.
Out of their coats
  They slipped right soon,
And neat and nicesome
  Put each his shoon.
One — Two — Three! —
  And away they go,
Not too fast,
  And not too slow;
Out from the elm-tree's
  Noonday shadow,
Into the sun
  And across the meadow.
Past the schoolroom,
  With knees well bent
Fingers a-flicking,
  They dancing went.
Up sides and over,
  And round and round,
They crossed click-clacking,
  The Parish bound,
By Tupman's meadow
  They did their mile,
Tee-to-tum

DOWN-ADOWN-DERRY

On a three-barred stile.
Then straight through Whipham,
    Downhill to Week,
Footing it lightsome,
    But not too quick,
Up fields to Watchet,
    And on through Wye,
Till seven fine churches
    They'd seen skip by —
Seven fine churches,
    And five old mills,
Farms in the valley,
    And sheep on the hills;
Old Man's Acre
    And Dead Man's Pool
All left behind,
    As they danced through Wool.
And Wool gone by,
    Like tops that seem
To spin in sleep
    They danced in dream:
Withy — Wellover —
    Wassop — Wo —
Like an old clock
    Their heels did go.
A league and a league
    And a league they went,
And not one weary,
    And not one spent.

And lo, and behold!
  Past Willow-cum-Leigh
Stretched with its waters
  The great green sea.
Says Farmer Bates,
  "I puffs and I blows,
What's under the water,
  Why, no man knows!"
Says Farmer Giles,
  "My wind comes weak,
And a good man drownded
  Is far to seek."
But Farmer Turvey,
  On twirling toes
Up's with his gaiters,
  And in he goes:
Down where the mermaids
  Pluck and play
On their twangling harps
  In a sea-green day;
Down where the mermaids,
  Finned and fair,
Sleek with their combs
  Their yellow hair. . . .
Bates and Giles —
  On the shingle sat,
Gazing at Turvey's
  Floating hat.
But never a ripple

Nor bubble told
Where he was supping
  Off plates of gold.
Never an echo
  Rilled through the sea
Of the feasting and dancing
  And minstrelsy.
They called — called — called:
  Came no reply:
Nought but the ripples'
  Sandy sigh.
Then glum and silent
  They sat instead,
Vacantly brooding
  On home and bed,
Till both together
  Stood up and said: —
"Us knows not, dreams not,
  Where you be,
Turvey, unless
  In the deep blue sea;
But excusing silver —
  And it comes most willing —
Here's us two paying
  Our forty shilling;
For it's sartin sure, Turvey,
  Safe and sound,
You danced us square, Turvey,
  Off the ground!"

SADLY, O, SADLY

SADLY, O, sadly, the sweet bells of Baddeley
Played in their steeples when Robin was gone,
Killed by an arrow,
Shot by Cock Sparrow,
Out of a Maybush, fragrant and wan.

DOWN – A DOWN – DERRY

Grievedly, grievedly, tolled distant Shieveley,
When the Dwarfs laid poor Snow-white asleep on the
hill,
Drowsed by an apple,
The Queen, sly and subtle,
Had cut with her knife on the blossomy sill.

THE DWARF

"Now, Jinnie, my dear, to the dwarf be off,
 That lives in Barberry Wood,
And fetch me some honey, but be sure you don't
  laugh, —
 He hates little girls that are rude, are rude,
 He hates little girls that are rude."

Jane tapped at the door of the house in the wood,
 And the dwarf looked over the wall,
He eyed her so queer, 'twas as much as she could
 To keep from laughing at all, at all,
 To keep from laughing at all.

His shoes down the passage came clod, clod, clod,
 And when he opened the door,
He croaked so harsh, 'twas as much as she could
 To keep from laughing the more, the more,
 To keep from laughing the more.

As there, with his bushy red beard, he stood,
 Pricked out to double its size,
He squinted so cross, 'twas as much as she could
 To keep the tears out of her eyes, her eyes,
 To keep the tears out of her eyes.

109

DOWN-ADOWN-DERRY

He slammed the door, and went clod, clod, clod,
  But while in the porch she bides,
He squealed so fierce, 'twas as much as she could
  To keep from cracking her sides, her sides,
    To keep from cracking her sides.

He threw a pumpkin over the wall,
  And melons and apples beside,
So thick in the air that to see them all fall,
  She laughed, and laughed, till she cried, cried, cried;
    Jane laughed and laughed till she cried.

Down fell her teardrops a-pit-a-pat-pat,
  And red as a rose she grew; —
"Kah! kah," said the dwarf, "is it crying you're at?
  It's the very worst thing you could do, do, do,
    It's the very worst thing you could do."

He slipped like a monkey up into a tree,
  He shook her down cherries like rain;
"See now," says he, cheeping, "a blackbird I be,
  Laugh, laugh, little Jinnie, again — gain — gain,
    Laugh, laugh, little Jinnie, again."

Ah me! what a strange, what a gladsome duet
  From a house in the deeps of a wood!
Such shrill and such harsh voices never met yet
  A-laughing as loud as they could, could, could,
    A-laughing as loud as they could.

110

DOWN-ADOWN-DERRY

Come Jinnie, come dwarf, cocksparrow, and bee,
   There's a ring gaudy-green in the dell,
Sing, sing, ye sweet cherubs, that flit in the tree;
   La! who can draw tears from a well, well, well,
   Who ever drew tears from a well!

LONGLEGS

LONGLEGS — he yelled "Coo-ee!"
  And all across the combe
Shrill and shrill it rang — rang through
  The clear green gloom.
Fairies there were a-spinning,
  And a white tree-maid
Lifted her eyes, and listened
  In her rain-sweet glade.
Bunnie to bunnie stamped; old Wat
  Chin-deep in bracken sate;
A throstle piped, "I'm by, I'm by!"
  Clear to his timid mate.
And there was Longlegs straddling,
  And hearkening was he,
To distant Echo thrilling back
  A thin "Coo-ee!"

THE MERMAIDS

SAND, sand; hills of sand;
  And the wind where nothing is
Green and sweet of the land;
  No grass, no trees,
  No bird, no butterfly,
But hills, hills of sand,
  And a burning sky.

Sea, sea, mounds of the sea,
  Hollow, and dark, and blue,
Flashing incessantly
  The whole sea through;
  No flower, no jutting root,
Only the floor of the sea,
  With foam afloat.

Blow, blow, winding shells;
  And the watery fish,
Deaf to the hidden bells,
  In the water splash;
No streaming gold, no eyes,
  Watching along the waves,
But far-blown shells, faint bells,
  From the darkling caves.

116

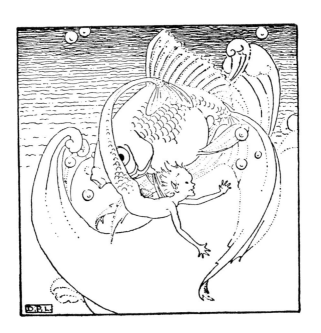

THE LITTLE CREATURE

TWINKUM, twankum, twirlum and twitch
My great grandam — She was a Witch.

119

DOWN-ADOWN-DERRY

Mouse in wainscot, Saint in niche —
My great grandam — She was a Witch;
Deadly nightshade flowers in a ditch —
My great grandam — She was a Witch;
Long though the shroud it grows stitch by stitch —
My great grandam — She was a Witch;
Wean your weakling before you breech —
My great grandam — She was a Witch;
The fattest pig's but a double flitch —
My great grandam — She was a Witch;
Nightjars rattle, owls scritch —
My great grandam — She was a Witch.

   Pretty and small,
   A mere nothing at all,
   Pinned up sharp in the ghost of a shawl,
   She'd straddle her down to the kirkyard wall,
   And mutter and whisper and call; and call —
   And — call.

Red blood out and black blood in,
My Nannie says I'm a child of sin —
How did I choose me my witchcraft kin!
Know I as soon as dark's dreams begin
Snared is my heart in a nightmare's gin;
Never from terror I out may win;
So dawn and dusk I pine, peak, thin,
Scarcely beknowing t'other from which —
My great grandam — She was a Witch.

SAM

WHEN Sam goes back in memory,
   It is to where the sea
Breaks on the shingle, emerald-green,
   In white foam, endlessly;
He says — with small brown eye on mine —
   "I used to keep awake,
And lean from my window in the moon,
   Watching those billows break.

DOWN-ADOWN-DERRY

And half a million tiny hands,
  And eyes, like sparks of frost,
Would dance and come tumbling into the moon,
  On every breaker tossed.
And all across from star to star,
  I've seen the watery sea,
With not a single ship in sight,
  Just ocean there, and me;
And heard my father snore. And once,
  As sure as I'm alive,
Out of those wallowing, moon-flecked waves
  I saw a mermaid dive;
Head and shoulders above the wave,
  Plain as I now see you,
Combing her hair, now back, now front,
  Her two eyes peeping through;
Calling me, 'Sam!' — quietlike — 'Sam!' . . .
  But me . . . I never went,
Making believe I kind of thought
  'Twas some one else she meant. . . .
Wonderful lovely there she sat,
  Singing the night away,
All in the solitudinous sea
  Of that there lonely bay."

"P'raps," and he'd smooth his hairless mouth,
  "P'raps, if 'twere now, my son,
P'raps, if I heard a voice say, 'Sam!' . . .
  Morning would find me gone."

DOWN-A DOWN-DERRY

THE WITCH

WEARY went the old Witch,
    Weary of her pack,
She sat her down by the churchyard wall,
    And jerked it off her back.

The cord brake, yes, the cord brake,
    Just where the dead did lie,
And Charms and Spells and Sorceries
    Spilled out beneath the sky.

Weary was the old Witch;
    She rested her old eyes
From the lantern-fruited yew trees,
    And the scarlet of the skies;

And out the dead came stumbling,
    From every rift and crack,
Silent as moss, and plundered
    The gaping pack.

They wish them, three times over,
    Away they skip full soon:
Bat and Mole and Leveret,
    Under the rising moon;

125

DOWN-ADOWN-DERRY

Owl and Newt and Nightjar:
    They take their shapes and creep,
Silent as churchyard lichen,
    While she squats asleep.

All of these dead were stirring:
    Each unto each did call,
"A Witch, a Witch is sleeping
    Under the churchyard wall;

"A Witch, a Witch is sleeping . . ."
    The shrillness ebbed away;
And up the way-worn moon clomb bright,
    Hard on the track of day.

She shone, high, wan and silvery;
    Day's colours paled and died:
And, save the mute and creeping worm,
    Nought else was there beside.

Names may be writ; and mounds rise;
    Purporting, Here be bones:
But empty is that churchyard
    Of all save stones.

Owl and Newt and Nightjar,
    Leveret, Bat and Mole
Haunt and call in the twilight,
    Where she slept, poor soul.

126

THE JOURNEY

HEART-SICK of his journey was the Wanderer;
  Footsore and parched was he;
And a Witch who long had lurked by the wayside,
  Looked out of sorcery.

"Lift up your eyes, you lonely Wanderer,"
  She peeped from her casement small;
"Here's shelter and quiet to give you rest, young man,
  And apples for thirst withal."

And he looked up out of his sad reverie,
  And saw all the woods in green,
With birds that flitted feathered in the dappling,
  The jewel-bright leaves between.

And he lifted up his face towards her lattice,
  And there, alluring-wise,
Slanting through the silence of the long past,
  Dwelt the still green Witch's eyes.

And vaguely from the hiding-place of memory
  Voices seemed to cry;
"What is the darkness of one brief life-time
  To the deaths thou hast made us die?"

129

DOWN-ADOWN-DERRY

"Heed not the words of the Enchantress
　Who would us still betray!"
And sad with the echo of their reproaches,
　Doubting, he turned away.

"I may not shelter 'neath your roof, lady,
　Nor in this wood's green shadow seek repose,
Nor will your apples quench the thirst
　A homesick wanderer knows."

"'Homesick, forsooth!'" she softly mocked him:
　And the beauty in her face
Made in the sunshine pale and trembling
　A stillness in that place.

And he sighed, as if in fear, the young Wanderer,
　Looking to left and to right,
Where the endless narrow road swept onward,
　In the distance lost to sight.

And there fell upon his sense the briar,
　Haunting the air with its breath,
And the faint shrill sweetness of the birds' throats,
　Their tent of leaves beneath.

And there was the Witch, in no wise heeding;
　Her arbour, and fruit-filled dish,
Her pitcher of well-water, and clear damask —
　All that the weary wish.

DOWN-ADOWN-DERRY

And the last gold beam across the green world
　Faltered and failed, as he
Remembered his solitude and the dark night's
　Inhospitality.

And he looked upon the Witch with eyes of sorrow
　In the darkening of the day;
And turned him aside into oblivion;
　And the voices died away. . . .

And the Witch stepped down from her casement:
　In the hush of night he heard
The calling and wailing in dewy thicket
　Of bird to hidden bird.

And gloom stole all her burning crimson,
　Remote and faint in space
As stars in gathering shadow of the evening
　Seemed now her phantom face.

And one night's rest shall be a myriad,
　Midst dreams that come and go;
Till heedless fate, unmoved by weakness, bring him
　This same strange by-way through:

To the beauty of earth that fades in ashes,
　The lips of welcome, and the eyes
More beauteous than the feeble shine of Hesper
　Lone in the lightening skies:

Till once again the Witch's guile entreat him;
  But, worn with wisdom, he
Steadfast and cold shall choose the dark night's
  Inhospitality.

AS LUCY WENT A-WALKING

As Lucy went a-walking one morning cold and fine,
There sate three crows upon a bough, and three times
    three is nine:
Then "O!" said Lucy, in the snow, "it's very plain to
    see
A witch has been a-walking in the fields in front
    of me."

Then stept she light and heedfully across the frozen
    snow,
And plucked a bunch of elder-twigs that near a pool did
    grow:
And, by and by, she comes to seven shadows in one
    place
Stretched black by seven poplar-trees against the sun's
    bright face.

She looks to left, she looks to right, and in the midst
    she sees
A little pool of water clear and frozen 'neath the
    trees;
Then down beside its margent in the crusty snow she
    kneels,
And hears a magic belfry a-ringing with sweet bells.

DOWN-ADOWN-DERRY

Clear sang the faint far merry peal, then silence on the air,
And icy-still the frozen pool and poplars standing there:
Then lo! as Lucy turned her head and looked along the
snow
She sees a witch — a witch she sees, come frisking to
and fro.

Her scarlet, buckled shoes they clicked, her heels a-
twinkling high;
With mistletoe her steeple-hat bobbed as she capered by;
But never a dint, or mark, or print, in the whiteness
for to see,
Though danced she high, though danced she fast, though
danced she lissomely.

It seemed 'twas diamonds in the air, or little flakes of
frost;
It seemed 'twas golden smoke around, or sunbeams
lightly tossed;
It seemed an elfin music like to reeds and warblers rose:
"Nay!" Lucy said, "it is the wind that through the
branches flows."

And as she peeps, and as she peeps, 'tis no more one,
but three,
And eye of bat, and downy wing of owl within the tree,
And the bells of that sweet belfry a-pealing as before
And now it is not three she sees, and now it is not
four —

"O! who are ye," sweet Lucy cries, "that in a dreadful
  ring,
All muffled up in brindled shawls, do caper, frisk, and
  spring?"
"A witch, and witches, one and nine," they straight to
  her reply,
And looked upon her narrowly, with green and needle
  eye.

Then Lucy sees in clouds of gold green cherry trees up-
  grow,
And bushes of red roses that bloomed above the snow;
She smells, all faint, the almond-boughs blowing so
  wild and fair
And doves with milky eyes ascend fluttering in the air.

Clear flowers she sees, like tulip buds, go floating by
  like birds,
With wavering tips that warbled sweetly strange enchanted words;
And, as with ropes of amethyst, the boughs with lamps
  were hung,
And clusters of green emeralds like fruit upon them
  clung.

"O witches nine, ye dreadful nine, O witches seven and
  three!
Whence come these wondrous things that I this Christmas morning see?"

DOWN-ADOWN-DERRY

But straight, as in a clap, when she of Christmas says
    the word,
Here is the snow, and there the sun, but never bloom
    nor bird;

Nor warbling flame, nor gleaming-rope of amethyst
    there shows,
Nor bunches of green emeralds, nor belfry, well, and
    rose,
Nor cloud of gold, nor cherry-tree, nor witch in brindle
    shawl,
But like a dream that vanishes, so vanished were they
    all.

When Lucy sees, and only sees three crows upon a
    bough,
And earthly twigs, and bushes hidden white in driven
    snow,
Then "O!" said Lucy, "three times three is nine — I
    plainly see
Some witch has been a-walking in the fields in front of
    me."

THE WORLD OF DREAM

BEWARE!

An ominous bird sang from its branch
  "Beware, O Wanderer!
Night 'mid her flowers of glamourie spilled
  Draws swiftly near:

"Night with her darkened caravans,
  Piled deep with silver and myrrh,
Draws from the portals of the East,
  O Wanderer near.

"Night who walks plumèd through the fields
  Of stars that strangely stir —
Smitten to fire by the sandals of him
  Who walks with her."

SOME ONE

SOME one came knocking
  At my wee, small door;
Some one came knocking,
  I'm sure — sure — sure;

DOWN-ADOWN-DERRY

I listened, I opened,
  I looked to left and right,
But nought there was a-stirring
  In the still dark night;
Only the busy beetle
  Tap-tapping in the wall,
Only from the forest
  The screech-owl's call,
Only the cricket whistling
  While the dewdrops fall,
So I know not who came knocking,
  At all, at all, at all.

MUSIC

WHEN music sounds, gone is the earth I know,
And all her lovely things even lovelier grow;
Her flowers in vision flame, her forest trees
Lift burdened branches, stilled with ecstasies.

When music sounds, out of the water rise
Naiads whose beauty dims my waking eyes,
Rapt in strange dreams burns each enchanted face,
With solemn echoing stirs their dwelling-place.

When music sounds, all that I was I am
Ere to this haunt of brooding dust I came;
While from Time's woods break into distant song
The swift-winged hours, as I haste along.

HAUNTED

THE rabbit in his burrow keeps
No guarded watch, in peace he sleeps;
The wolf that howls in challenging night
Cowers to her lair at morning light;
The simplest bird entwines a nest
Where she may lean her lovely breast,
Couched in the silence of the bough.
But thou, O man, what rest hast thou?

149

DOWN-A DOWN-DERRY

Thy emptiest solitude can bring
Only a subtler questioning
In thy divided heart. Thy bed
Recalls at dawn what midnight said.
Seek how thou wilt to feign content,
Thy flaming ardour's quickly spent;
Soon thy last company is gone,
And leaves thee — with thyself — alone.

Pomp and great friends may hem thee round,
A thousand busy tasks be found;
Earth's thronging beauties may beguile
Thy longing lovesick heart awhile;
And pride, like clouds of sunset, spread
A changing glory round thy head;
But fade will all; and thou must come,
Hating thy journey, homeless, home.

Rave how thou wilt; unmoved, remote,
That inward presence slumbers not,
Frets out each secret from thy breast,
Gives thee no rally, pause, nor rest,
Scans close thy very thoughts, lest they
Should sap his patient power away,
Answers thy wrath with peace, thy cry
With tenderest taciturnity.

THEY TOLD ME

THEY told me Pan was dead, but I
  Oft marvelled who it was that sang
Down the green valleys languidly
  Where the grey elder-thickets hang.

151

DOWN-ADOWN-DERRY

Sometimes I thought it was a bird
  My soul had charged with sorcery;
Sometimes it seemed my own heart heard
  Inland the sorrow of the sea.

But even where the primrose sets
  The seal of her pale loveliness,
I found amid the violets
  Tears of an antique bitterness.

THE SUNKEN GARDEN

SPEAK not — whisper not;
Here bloweth thyme and bergamot;
Softly on the evening hour,
Secret herbs their spices shower.
Dark-spiked rosemary and myrrh,
Lean-stalked, purple lavender;
Hides within her bosom, too,
All her sorrows, bitter rue.

153

DOWN-ADOWN-DERRY

Breathe not — trespass not;
Of this green and darkling spot,
Latticed from the moon's beams,
Perchance a distant dreamer dreams;
Perchance upon its darkening air,
The unseen ghosts of children fare,
Faintly swinging, sway and sweep,
Like lovely sea-flowers in its deep;
While, unmoved, to watch and ward,
Amid its gloomed and daisied sward,
Stands with bowed and dewy head
That one little leaden Lad.

SNOW

No breath of wind,
No gleam of sun —
Still the white snow
Swirls softly down —
Twig and bough
And blade and thorn
All in an icy
Quiet, forlorn.
Whispering, nestling,
Through the air,
On sill and stone,
Roof — everywhere,
It heaps its powdery
Crystal flakes,
Of every tree
A mountain makes:
Till pale and faint
At shut of day,
Stoops from the West
One wintry ray.
Then, feathered in fire,
Where ghosts the moon,

DOWN-ADOWN-DERRY

A robin shrills
His lonely tune;
And from her dark-gnarled
Yew-tree lair
Flits she who had been
In hiding there.

THE WORLD OF DREAM

Now, through the dusk
With muffled bell

DOWN-ADOWN-DERRY

The Dustman comes
   The World to tell,
Night's elfin lanterns
   Burn and gleam
In the twilight, wonderful
   World of Dream.

Hollow and dim
   Sleep's boat doth ride,
Heavily still
   At the waterside.
Patter, patter,
   The children come,
Yawning and sleepy,
   Out of the gloom.

Like droning bees
   In a garden green,
Over the thwarts
   They clamber in.
And lovely Sleep
   With long-drawn oar
Turns away
   From the whispering shore.

Over the water
   Like roses glide
Her hundreds of passengers
   Packed inside,

DOWN-ADOWN-DERRY

To where in her garden
Tremble and gleam
The harps and lamps
Of the World of Dream.

QUEEN DJENIRA

WHEN Queen Djenira slumbers through
  The sultry noon's repose,
From out her dreams, as soft she lies,
  A faint thin music flows.

Her lovely hands lie narrow and pale
  With gilded nails, her head
Couched in its banded nets of gold
  Lies pillowed on her bed.

The little Nubian boys who fan
  Her cheeks and tresses clear,
Wonderful, wonderful, wonderful voices
  Seem afar to hear.

They slide their eyes, and nodding, say,
  "Queen Djenira walks to-day
The courts of the lord Pthamasar
  Where the sweet birds of Psuthys are."

And those of earth about her porch
  Of shadow cool and grey
Their sidelong beaks in silence lean,
  And silent flit away.

NIGHTFALL

THE last light fails — that shallow pool of day!
The coursers of the dark stamp down to drink,
Arch their wild necks, lift their wild heads and neigh;
Their drivers, gathering at the water-brink,
With eyes ashine from out their clustering hair,
Utter their hollow speech, or gaze afar,
Rapt in irradiant reverie, to where
Languishes, lost in light, the evening star.

DOWN-ADOWN-DERRY

Come the wood-nymphs to dance within the glooms,
Calling these charioteers with timbrels' din;
Ashen with twilight the dark forest looms
O'er the nocturnal beasts that prowl within
"O glory of beauty which the world makes fair!"
Pant they their serenading on the air.

Sound the loud hooves, and all abroad the sky
The lusty charioteers their stations take;
Planet to planet do the sweet Loves fly,
And in the zenith silver music wake.
Cities of men, in blindness hidden low,
Fume their faint flames to that arched firmament,
But all the dwellers in the lonely know
The unearthly are abroad, and weary and spent,
With rush extinguished, to their dreaming go.
And world and night and star-enclustered space
The glory of beauty are in one enravished face.

CUMBERLAND

The old, old King of Cumberland
　　Awoke with bristling beard —
Crouched listening in the darkness
　　To a sound that he had heard.

He leaned upon his foursquare bed,
　　His thumb beneath his chin;
Hearkening after that which had stirred
　　The dream that he was in.

The old, old King of Cumberland
　　Muttered, " Twas not the sea,
Gushing upon Shlievlisskin rocks,
　　That wakened me.

"Thunder from midmost night it was not;
　　For yonder at the bars
Burn to their summer setting her
　　Clear constellated stars."

The old, old King of Cumberland
　　Mused yet, "Rats ever did
Rove from their holes, and clink my spurs,
　　And gnaw my coverlid.

DOWN-ADOWN-DERRY

"Oft hath a little passing breeze
  Along this valance stirred;
But in this stagnant calm 'twas not
  The wind I heard.

"Some keener, stranger, quieter, closer
  Voice it was me woke. . . ."
And silence, like a billow, drowned
  The word he spoke.

His chamber walls were cloaked with dark;
  Shadow did thickly brood,
And in the vague, all-listening night
  A presence stood. . . .

Sudden a gigantic hand he thrust
  Into his bosom cold,
Where now no surging restless beat
  Its long tale told:

Swept on him then, as there he sate,
  Terror icy chill;
'Twas silence that had him awoke —
  His heart stood still.

THE LITTLE GREEN ORCHARD

SOME one is always sitting there,
              In the little green orchard;
  Even when the sun is high
  In noon's unclouded sky,
  And faintly droning goes
  The bee from rose to rose,
Some one in shadow is sitting there,
              In the little green orchard.

171

DOWN-ADOWN-DERRY

Yes, and when twilight is falling softly
          In the little green orchard;
     When the grey dew distils
     And every flower-cup fills;
     When the last blackbird says,
     "What — what!" and goes her way — s-sh!
I have heard voices calling softly
          In the little green orchard.

Not that I am afraid of being there,
          In the little green orchard;
     Why, when the moon's been bright,
     Shedding her lonesome light,
     And moths like ghosties come,
     And the horned snail leaves home:
I've sat there, whispering and listening there,
          In the little green orchard.

Only it's strange to be feeling there,
          In the little green orchard;
     Whether you paint or draw,
     Dig, hammer, chop, or saw;
     When you are most alone,
     All but the silence gone . . .
Some one is waiting and watching there,
          In the little green orchard.

172

THE TRUANTS

ERE my heart beats too coldly and faintly
  To remember sad things, yet be gay,
I would sing a brief song of the world's little children
  Magic hath stolen away.

The primroses scattered by April,
  The stars of the wide Milky Way,
Cannot outnumber the hosts of the children
  Magic hath stolen away.

The buttercup green of the meadows,
  The snow of the blossoming may,
Lovelier are not than the legions of children
  Magic hath stolen away.

173

DOWN-A DOWN-DERRY

The waves tossing surf in the moonbeam,
   The albatross lone on the spray,
Alone know the tears wept in vain for the children
   Magic hath stolen away.

In vain: for at hush of the evening
   When the stars twinkle into the grey,
Seems to echo the far-away calling of children
   Magic hath stolen away.

THE LITTLE SALAMANDER

TO MARGOT

WHEN I go free,
I think 'twill be
A night of stars and snow,
And the wild fires of frost shall light
My footsteps as I go;
Nobody — nobody will be there
With groping touch, or sight,
To see me in my bush of hair
Dance burning through the night.

VOICES

WHO is it calling by the darkened river
   Where the moss lies smooth and deep,
And the dark trees lean unmoving arms,
   Silent and vague in sleep,
And the bright-heeled constellations pass
   In splendour through the gloom;
Who is it calling o'er the darkened river
     In music, "Come!"?

Who is it wandering in the summer meadows
   Where the children stoop and play
In the green faint-scented flowers, spinning
   The guileless hours away?
Who touches their bright hair? who puts
   A wind-shell to each cheek,
Whispering betwixt its breathing silences,
     "Seek! seek!"?

Who is it watching in the gathering twilight
   When the curfew bird hath flown
On eager wings, from song to silence,
   To its darkened nest alone?
Who takes for brightening eyes the stars,
   For locks the still moonbeam,
Sighs through the dews of evening peacefully
     Falling, "Dream!"

SORCERY

"WHAT voice is that I hear
    Crying across the pool?"
"It is the voice of Pan you hear,
Crying his sorceries shrill and clear,
    In the twilight dim and cool."

"What song is it he sings,
    Echoing from afar;
While the sweet swallow bends her wings,
Filling the air with twitterings,
    Beneath the brightening star?"

The woodman answered me,
    His faggot on his back: —
"Seek not the face of Pan to see;
Flee from his clear note summoning thee
    To darkness deep and black!

"He dwells in thickest shade,
    Piping his notes forlorn
Of sorrow never to be allayed;
Turn from his coverts sad
    Of twilight unto morn!"

DOWN-A DOWN-DERRY

The woodman passed away
  Along the forest path;
His ax shone keen and grey
In the last beams of day:
  And all was still as death: —

Only Pan singing sweet
  Out of Earth's fragrant shade;
I dreamed his eyes to meet,
  And found but shadow laid
Before my tired feet.

Comes no more dawn to me,
  Nor bird of open skies.
Only his woods' deep gloom I see
  Till, at the end of all, shall rise,
Afar and tranquilly,
Death's stretching sea.

MELMILLO

THREE and thirty birds there stood
In an elder in a wood;
Called Melmillo — flew off three,
Leaving thirty in a tree;
Called Melmillo — nine now gone,
And the boughs held twenty-one;
Called Melmillo — eighteen
Left but three to nod and preen;
Called Melmillo — three — two — one —
Now of birds were feathers none.

Then stole slim Melmillo in
To that wood all dusk and green,
And with lean long palms outspread
Softly a strange dance did tread;
Not a note of music she
Had for echoing company;
All the birds were flown to rest
In the hollow of her breast;
In the wood thorn, elder, willow —
Danced alone — lone danced Melmillo.

THE QUIET ENEMY

HEARKEN! now the hermit bee
Drones a quiet threnody;
Greening on the stagnant pool
The criss-cross light is beautiful;
In the venomed yew tree wings
Preen and flit. The linnet sings.

Gradually the brave sun
Sinks to a day's journey done;
In the marshy flats abide
Mists to muffle midnight-tide.
Puffed within the belfry tower
Hungry owls drowse out their hour. . .

Walk in beauty. Vaunt thy rose.
Flaunt thy poisonous loveliness!
Pace for pace with thee there goes
A shape that hath not come to bless.
I, thine enemy? . . . Nay, nay!
I can only watch, and wait
Patient treacherous time away,
Hold ajar the wicket gate.

188

MISTLETOE

Sitting under the mistletoe
(Pale-green, fairy mistletoe),
One last candle burning low,
All the sleepy dancers gone,
Just one candle burning on,
Shadows lurking everywhere:
Some one came, and kissed me there.

191

DOWN-ADOWN-DERRY

Tired I was; my head would go
Nodding under the mistletoe
(Pale-green, fairy mistletoe),
No footsteps came, no voice, but only,
Just as I sat there, sleepy, lonely,
Stooped in the still and shadowy air
Lips unseen — and kissed me there.

NOT I

As I came out of Wiseman's Street,
The air was thick with driving sleet;
Crossing over Proudman's Square,
Cold clouds and louring dulled the air;
But as I turned to Goodman's Lane,
The burning sun came out again;
And on the roof of Children's Row
In solemn glory shone the snow.
There did I lodge; there hope to die:
Envying no man — no, not I.

Made in United States
North Haven, CT
28 March 2022